# Just Like You, Little Lamb

Written by Melissa Dallke

# Acknowledgments

I want to thank the Lord, for everything.

A special thanks to my daughter Phoebe for the beautiful photography in this book.

Thank you to my husband Brice for completely supporting me through this whole process!

I want to thank my children BJ, Phoebe, Clara, Benjamin, and Allison. Watching you play and curling up reading countless books with you is what inspired everything behind this book.

And to our families' two newest additions: our grandchildren Arianna and Trey!

*She seeks wool and flax, and works with willing hands.*
*Proverbs 31:13 (ESV)*

# Just Like You, Little Lamb

Little lamb was born early
on a bright spring morning.
His mommy kept him cozy with her soft wool.
He even drank warm milk...

...just like you did as a baby!

At first little lamb had wobbly legs...

...just like you!

Soon, little lamb grew.
Now he could run and play outside.
He loved playing in the summer sun...

...just like you!

The seasons passed,
and little lamb kept growing.

Now he loved playing in the crunchy autumn leaves.

Just like you!

The autumn days turned into winter.

Little lamb grew even bigger.
He was so big now that
his own wool kept him warm.

Soon, it was spring again
and it was time for little lamb to be sheared.
That is a haircut for sheep.
Did you know that sheep get haircuts?

Just like you!

Guess what little lamb's
wool will become...

Yarn!

People use yarn to make hats,
sweaters, socks, toys,
and so much more!

Just for you!

# Little Lamb Instructions

## Materials

Cascade 220 Heathers Worsted Weight or similar worsted weight yarn

100% Peruvian Highland Wool

1 ball of Antiqued Heather (white)

1 ball of Doeskin Heather (brown)

Scraps of worsted weight pink for inner ear (I dyed a little of the white)

Scraps of worsted weight dark brown for eyes


## Tools

US size 4 set of four double pointed needles

Stitch markers

Yarn needle

Polyester fiberfill

*Gauge is not important; just make sure your stitches are close enough that the stuffing will not show through.*


## Finished Measurements

Head circumference from nose going around back of head: 9 ½ inches

Height from top of head to bottom hoof: about 10 ¾ inches

Body circumference: 9 inches around middle


## Head

With Doeskin Heather (brown), cast on 6 stitches, placing 2 stitches on each of the three double pointed needles. Join to work in the round, being careful not to twist the stitches. Place a stitch marker on the first stitch. We will be working from the nose to the back of the head.

Rnd 1- k1 in each st (6)

Rnd 2- kfb in each st (12)

Rnd 3- (k1, kfb) repeat across the round (18)

Rnd 4- k1 in each st

Rnd 5- (k2, kfb) repeat across the round (24)

Rnd 6-9- k1 in each st

Rnd 10- (k3, kfb) repeat across the round (30)

Rnd 11- k1 in each st

Rnd 12- (k4, kfb) repeat across the round (36)

Rnd 13- k1 in each st

Change to Antiqued Heather (white)

Rnd 14- k1 in each st

Rnd 15- (k5, kfb) repeat across the round (42)

Rnd 16-26- k1 in each st

Rnd 27- (k5, k2 tog) repeat across the round (36)

Rnd 28- k1 in each st

Rnd 29- (k4, k2 tog) repeat across the round (30)

Rnd 30- k1 in each st

Rnd 31- (k3, k2 tog) repeat across the round (24)

Rnd 32- k1 in each st

Begin stuffing the head.

Rnd 33- (k2, k2 tog) repeat across the round (18)

Rnd 34- k1 in each st

Rnd 35- (k1, k2 tog) repeat across the round (12)

Rnd 36- (k2 tog) repeat across the round (6)

Finish stuffing the head. Cut the yarn and thread the tail on a yarn needle, pull through the remaining stitches and gather up tight to close the hole.

Body

Leaving a long tail, cast on 6 stitches with Antiqued Heather (white). Placing 2 stitches on three double pointed needles. Join to work in the round, being careful not to twist the stitches. Place a stitch marker on the first stitch.

Rnd 1- k1 in each st (6)

Rnd 2- kfb in each st (12)

Rnd 3- (k1, kfb) repeat across the round (18)

Rnd 4- k1 in each st

Rnd 5- (k2, kfb) repeat across the round (24)

Rnd 6- k1 in each st

Rnd 7- (k3, kfb) repeat across the round (30)

Rnd 8- k1 in each st

Rnd 9- (k4, kfb) repeat across the round (36)

Rnd 10- k1 in each st

Rnd 11- (k5, kfb) repeat across the round (42)

Rnd 12-18- k1 in each st

Rnd 19- (k6, kfb) repeat across the round (48)

Rnd 20- k1 in each st

Rnd 21- (k7, kfb) repeat across the round (54)

Rnds 22-39- k1 in each st

Rnd 40- (k7, k2 tog) repeat across the round (48)

Rnd 41- k1 in each st

Rnd 42- (k6, k2 tog) repeat across the round (42)

Rnd 43- k1 in each st

Rnd 44- (k5, k2 tog) repeat across the round (36)

Rnd 45- k1 in each st

Rnd 46- (k4, k2 tog) repeat across the round (30)

Rnd 47- k1 in each st

Begin stuffing body.

Rnd 48- (k3, k2 tog) repeat across the round (24)

Rnd 49- k1 in each st

Rnd 50- (k2, k2 tog) repeat across the round (18)

Rnd 51- k1 in each st

Rnd 52- (k1, k2 tog) repeat across the round (12)

Rnd 53- (k2 tog) repeat across the round (6)

Finish stuffing the body. Cut the yarn and thread the tail on a yarn needle. Pull through the remaining stitches and pull tight to close the hole.


Legs (make 4)

Leaving a long tail, cast on 8 stitches in Antiqued Heather (white). Three stitches on two needles and two stitches on one needle. Join to work in the round, being careful not to twist the stitches. Place a stitch marker on the first stitch. We will begin with the top of the leg, working our way down to the hoof.

Rnd 1- k1 in each st

Rnd 2- kfb in each st (16)

Rnd 3-24- k1 in each st

Rnd 25- (k1, kfb) repeat across the round (24)

Rnd 26- k1 in each st

Change to Doeskin Heather (brown)

Rnd 27- (k2, kfb) repeat across the round (32)

Rnd 28-38- k1 in each st

Rnd 39- (k2, k2 tog) repeat across the round (24)

Rnd 40- k1 in each st

Lightly begin stuffing the leg. Do not stuff the top of the leg where it will join to the body. Firmly stuff the hooves.

Rnd 41- (k1, k2 tog) repeat across the round (16)

Rnd 42- (k2 tog) repeat across the round (8)

Cut the yarn and thread the tail on a yarn needle. Pull through the remaining stitches and pull tight to close the hole.


Tail

Leaving a long tail, cast on 6 stitches in Antiqued Heather (white). Place two stitches on three double pointed needles. Join to work in the round, being careful not to twist the stitches. Place a stitch marker on the first stitch.

Rnd 1- k1 in each st

Rnd 2- kfb in each st (12)

Rnd 3-9- k1 in each st

Bind off, leaving a long tail for sewing to the body. Lightly stuff, thread yarn needle with cast on tail, and close the hole at the tip.


Ears (Make two from Antiqued Heather (white) yarn and two from pink yarn)

Using two double pointed needles and leaving a long tail, cast 6 stitches onto one needle.

R1 (and all odd numbered rows)- p1 in each st

R2- k1 in each st

R4- k1 in each st

R6- k1, kfb, k2, kfb, k1

R8- k1 in each st

R10- k1 in each st

R12- k1, ssk, k2, k2 tog, k1

R14- k1, ssk, k2 tog, k1

R16- ssk, k2 tog

Cut the yarn and thread tail on a yarn needle. Pull through the remaining stitches. Weave in end. Using cast on tail, thread on a yarn needle. Place one white ear and one pink ear together with right sides facing out and wrong sides (purl sides) together. Fold the bottom of ear together to form a cupping shape and stitch together. Continue to stitch around the ear using the mattress stitch.

Whipstitch head to body. Now whipstitch legs, tail, and ears to lamb using the photos as a guide.

With the dark brown scrap yarn, embroider eyes on the head.

# About the Author

Melissa is an indie yarn dyer, knit/crochet designer (softies are a favorite) and needlefelter! When she isn't surrounded in fluffy wool she is homeschooling and enjoying time with her family in the beautiful Flint Hills.

Made in the USA
Columbia, SC
16 December 2018